MY TINY PET ELEPHANT

From the Imagination of **Jessica Dailey**

Illustrated by Gabby Correia

Dedication

This book is dedicated to my three brilliant children William,
Izzabella, & Charlotte. I feel so lucky to be your mother and
to be able to experience childhood through your eyes.
You inspire me in so many ways, including this book.
I will love you all—more than you will ever know.

www.jessdailey.com

ISBN: 979-8-9852085-2-8 (Softcover)
979-8-9852085-0-4 (Hardcover)
979-8-9852085-3-5 (Ebook)
979-8-9852085-1-1 (Boardbook)

Dear tiny Adventurer,

The imagination knows no limits.
Remember that you have the unique gift
of making a thought become a reality.
Your mind is a wonderous place full of beautiful
things just waiting to be discovered.
Even the tiniest of dreams
can become the biggest adventure!
I hope it sparks your own imagination to run wild.
Thank you for sharing this tiny adventure with me!

With Kindness & Love,
Jess Dailey, COTA/L

If I could choose
any tiny pet,
it would be
a tiny pet...

Elephant!

So tiny, he would happily fit in the palms of my hands.

So tiny, his little **elephant** trunk would tickle my nose with sweet elephant kisses.

Everyday, my tiny pet
elephant would join me
for breakfast in the morning.

My mom wouldn't mind his tiny pet elephant messes

12

Then, after breakfast, my tiny pet **elephant** would help me get ready for our day.

I would bring my tiny pet **elephant** to school, where I would teach him tiny pet elephant tricks.

In the afternoon, we would
play fun games together.
So tiny, my pet elephant,
that he would win
Hide and Seek every time!

I would build him his very own tiny pet village where he could do tiny pet things.

At night, my tiny pet **elephant** would snuggle up close to me for a bedtime story.

The sound of his tiny
elephant horn wishes
me a gentle goodnight.
As I drift to sleep, I whisper,

"I love you my tiny pet **elephant**".

23

Did You Know?

10 FUN ELEPHANT FACTS

1. Elephants are the world's largest land animal.
2. Elephant tusks are actually their teeth.
3. Baby elephants are called calves and can walk within an hour after their birth.
4. Elephants love to eat and spend about sixteen hours a day eating.
5. Elephants can use their trunks to breathe under water.
6. Female elephants are pregnant for about two years.
7. Elephants use mud as sunscreen.
8. Elephants are afraid of bees.
9. Elephants travel in a herd.
10. Elephants are 'keystone species." It means they take care of the place where they live, maintaining pathways and access to water.

PARENT/CLASSROOM PROMPTS & INTERACTIVE ACTIVITIES

Designed for promoting cognitive development while encouraging gross-motor, fine-motor, play, and social skills.

Ask your child/ class the following questions for engaging in a fun conversation to spark their imagination while developing Play and Social Skills:

1 If you could have any tiny pet, what would you choose, and why?

2 What would you name your tiny pet?

3 Can you draw a picture of your tiny pet?

4 What fun things would you do with your tiny pet?

5 What fun tricks would you teach your tiny pet?

Fun activities for developing play, motor planning, and gross-motor skills:

ANIMAL WALKS

Pretending to be an animal can increase hand and body strength and encourage bilateral coordination while improving spatial awareness, fine- and gross-motor skills, direction-following, and motor planning. Animal walks are weight-bearing activities that provide proprioceptive input (inside the joints) and vestibular input (for the sense of balance in the inner ear). So, these are great activities to help kids calm themselves and improve their self-regulation skills.

ELEPHANT WALK

Prompt: *Let's walk like a tiny elephant!*
How: Get on all fours. Bend forward to place hands on the floor. Move your right hand and your right foot at the same time. Then, move your left hand and your left foot at the same time. Now, it's time for a tiny elephant trumpet! Lift your right hand in the air while making a trumpeting sound like a tiny elephant.
Get ready to repeat all the steps.

BUILD YOUR OWN TINY PET VILLAGE

Let's get creative with a STEM project. Use anything you can find around the house with permission from your parents first!
It could be cereal boxes, newspapers, a deck of cards, rulers, and so much more!

The Tiny Pet Elephant Village was made from:
A bottle cap, paper towel rolls, small boxes, tape, paper, art supplies, toothpicks, toys, and toilet tissue rolls.

SEARCH AND FIND

Find the many places our tiny pet elephant friend is hiding on page 16.

Can you find the seven places where he is hiding?

While searching during this activity, have the child use their pointer finger or another isolated finger to help them improve their fine motor and visual perception skills.

27

Made in the USA
Monee, IL
21 November 2023

46999598R00017